Happy Birthday

"Look — kittens!" Stephanie cried.

In the window, a crowd of kittens climbed and leaped and stalked — long-haired, short-haired, in every color from black to orange to gray.

"Hey — a calico! That's it!" I exclaimed.

"What's it?" said Stephanie.

"The perfect birthday present for Kate!" I said. "A calico kitten!"

Look for these and other books
in the Sleepover Friends Series:

Kate's Surprise

Susan Saunders

AN
APPLE
PAPERBACK

SCHOLASTIC INC.
New York Toronto London Auckland Sydney

ISBN 0-590-40643-4

12 11 10 9 8 7 6 5   9/8 0 1 2 3/9

Printed in the U.S.A.   11

Chapter
1

Kate Beekman turned on the blender and let it whirl for a few seconds. When the stuff inside looked like green paste, she turned the blender off. "That takes care of the avocado," she told us. "What's next?"

Stephanie Green studied the book she was holding. "Let's see — 'Add one cup of heavy cream. . . ,' " she read.

"Patti, would you look in the refrigerator?" Kate asked.

Patti Jenkins opened the Beekmans' double-doored refrigerator and moved things around on the shelves. "No heavy cream," she reported. "But there *is* some half-and-half."

Stephanie nodded. "That should be okay."

Kate measured out a cup of half-and-half and dumped it in the blender. "Anything else?"

"One egg," Stephanie answered.

Kate broke an egg into the blender, too. She turned it on again and left it running until the mixture was a smooth, pale green. Kate took the top off the blender and poured the avocado mixture into a bowl.

"It looks yummy." I tried to stick my finger into the bowl for a taste, but Kate snatched it away.

"Stop it, Lauren! Once you get started, there won't be any left for the rest of us," she scolded. "Let's take it upstairs."

Stephanie, Patti, and I — I'm Lauren Hunter — were at Kate's house for our Friday night sleepover. Kate and I live two houses down from each other on Pine Street. We've been best friends since kindergarten, which is when the sleepovers started. In those days, it was just the two of us — Kate's dad named us the Sleepover Twins.

Then Stephanie's family moved from the city to the other end of Pine Street. She and I got to be friends because we were in the same class in fourth grade. Stephanie started coming to the sleepovers, too, and having us stay overnight at her house.

Stephanie already had her own way of doing things, and Kate had *hers*, which led to some disagreements at first. Since I was friends with both of them, I'd find myself caught in the middle — at least until Patti moved to town.

Small world — Patti had known Stephanie in kindergarten and first grade back in the city. Although they hadn't seen each other in years, they both ended up in Mrs. Mead's fifth-grade class at Riverhurst Elementary, along with Kate and me. It wasn't long before Patti was the fourth member of the Sleepover Friends.

Kate switched off the light in the kitchen. "Quiet — Melissa!" she hissed as we followed her up the stairs.

Melissa — better known as Melissa the Monster — is Kate's little sister. There's nothing Melissa likes better than an excuse to crash our sleepover, unless it's getting us into trouble. And she has the sharpest ears around. We jumped over the really creaky step near the top and made it safely past her bedroom to Kate's room.

Kate closed the door and put the bowl down on the floor next to our tray of snacks: her special marshmallow fudge, my onion-soup-olives-bacon-bits-and-sour-cream dip, a basket of barbecue potato chips, and a giant-size bottle of Dr. Pepper.

"Dig in," Stephanie directed.

3

As I reached for the bowl, she added, "Try to remember, Lauren: your *face*, not your mouth!"

The four of us stuck our hands into the avocado mixture . . . and smeared it on our cheeks.

"Yuck!" Kate said, spreading a fingerful of green glop down her nose. "What is this supposed to do, exactly?"

"Give you taut skin and a glowing complexion," Stephanie replied, rubbing the goo across her chin. "The natural way to natural beauty," she added, pointing to the book she'd been reading in the kitchen. "I just wish your mother had had some honey, Kate."

"What for?" I asked, licking a little of the green goop off my finger. "Not bad," I murmured to Patti.

"You mix honey with herbs and lemon juice and use it as a conditioner for your hair," Stephanie answered.

"Maybe *you* do," Kate said to her. "But if you think I'm going to rub honey in *my* hair. . . ."

Stephanie reached into the bowl. "You missed a spot," she said, dabbing more avocado gunk on Kate's upper lip and shutting her up at the same time.

"How long do we have to leave it on?" Patti asked.

"Till it hardens," Stephanie said. "I guess about an hour."

4

"What time is it?" I peered out the window toward my house. From what I could see, no lights were on downstairs.

"After ten," Patti answered.

"What time is Roger bringing Linda back?" Stephanie wanted to know.

Roger is my older brother, and Linda's his girlfriend. "They had dinner reservations for eight o'clock at the Gilded Lobster. So it shouldn't be long now."

"I love surprise parties!" Stephanie said. "My seventh birthday party was a surprise. There's this restaurant in the city — "

"I think they're corny," Kate interrupted.

Stephanie looked at Patti and me and raised an eyebrow. Kate's own birthday was coming up in a couple of weeks, and it just so happened that Stephanie, Patti, and I were planning a surprise party!

"Oh, yeah?" Stephanie said. "What do you mean, exactly?"

"I'm sure Linda figured it out ages ago, and all of those people are sitting in Lauren's living room in the dark for nothing!" Kate declared.

"I bet Linda doesn't suspect a thing!" I replied.

"Well, *I* certainly would have caught on by now." Kate sniffed. "Doesn't Linda think it's kind of strange

5

that Roger's bringing her to your house at ten o'clock at night, in the middle of a date?"

"Roger's telling her that Mom made a cake especially for her. Besides, it's not officially Linda's birthday until Tuesday, so she won't be expecting anyone but my parents."

Stephanie looked out the window. "I love it when the lights suddenly go on, everybody yells 'Surprise!' and jumps out from behind doors. . . ." She turned to me with a big grin on her face. "Hey — maybe we can see it!"

I shook my head. "The Fosters' house is in the way."

"No — I mean *really* see it. Sneak over and look through the living room window — just until Linda gets her big surprise."

"In our pajamas?" Patti said, startled.

"Think of them as jogging outfits," Stephanie replied, looking down at hers. Stephanie's pajamas were striped red, black, and white, her favorite color combination.

"Roger would kill me!" I said.

"Not to mention my parents!" said Kate. "And what about the green faces?" She touched her avocado mask, which was still gooey.

Stephanie has an answer for everything. "Nobody's going to see us — we'll sneak down the alley and hide in the bushes in Lauren's yard." She glanced at Kate out of the corner of her eye. "Unless you're scared to."

Stephanie was turning it into a dare. "Truth or Dare" is one of our favorite sleepover activities — nobody turns down a dare.

"Who's scared?" Kate huffed. "Oh, come on!"

Luckily, Dr. Beekman had worked late in the hospital emergency room the night before. Kate's parents were already in their bedroom with the door closed. We pulled on our shoes and threw on jackets. Then we tiptoed downstairs again, through the kitchen, and out the back door. We left it open a crack, so we could get back inside in a hurry if we had to.

"The moon's like a spotlight!" Patti whispered.

It was so bright that our long, skinny shadows marched in front of us across the lawn. I stepped on a dry twig and jumped a mile. Patti and I giggled.

"Sssh — Donald's still awake," Kate murmured as she pushed through the hedge between her house and the Fosters'. "The light is on in his bedroom."

Donald Foster is probably the most conceited boy in Riverhurst, at least if you don't count the ones in high school. He's got blond hair and green eyes, and he thinks every girl in town is after him.

7

Since he lives between Kate and me, Donald has seen all of us in some pretty weird situations, like the time we couldn't wash the purple styling gel out of our hair because there was no water. I would be just as happy if he didn't get a look at us in our green avocado masks, though.

Keeping an eye on Donald's window, third from the end, we crept across the Fosters' backyard. Then we slipped into the alley. Before I opened my own gate, I warned everybody, "No matter what, we can't make any noise. Roger will strangle me if he finds out I'm snooping."

"I think I hear a car coming!" Patti whispered.

We stood still and listened. The car was moving up the street, getting closer. The engine rattled a little. . . .

"It sounds like Roger's car!" I whispered. "Hurry!"

The four of us scurried across the yard and crouched down in the lilacs next to the living room window. The car slowed down to turn into the driveway. The beams of the headlights swung over our heads.

"Keep down!" I warned.

"It's them!" Stephanie giggled.

"Sssh!" everybody else scolded.

The car stopped with a squeak of brakes, and

Roger climbed out. He walked around to open the passenger door for Linda.

"The house is awfully dark," we heard Linda say. "Maybe your parents are already in bed. Why don't we have the cake tomorrow, Roger?"

"You think she doesn't know what's up?!" Kate hissed.

I jabbed her in the ribs.

"Ouch!"

"Sssh!" Stephanie said.

"Er . . . uh . . . no! I'm sure they're . . . uh . . . just waiting for us to get here," Roger fumbled. "Let's go inside."

Stephanie started to get the nervous giggles again. Kate and I elbowed her hard to keep quiet.

Roger and Linda walked up to the front door. Roger opened it, and Linda stepped inside. . . .

The living room lights flashed on. About twenty high-school kids jumped out of the coat closet and from behind the couch. "Surprise! Surprise!" they shouted.

"Eeeeeh!" Linda screamed, before everybody started laughing and talking at once.

"Did you see how surprised she was? Linda didn't have a clue!" Stephanie whispered triumphantly to Kate.

9

As we watched, Mom walked into the living room from the kitchen. She was carrying a big white birthday cake ringed with lighted pink candles, and everyone was singing, "Happy birthday to you, happy birthday to you."

At that point, Bullwinkle joined in. Bullwinkle is our dog — Roger's dog, really, since Roger picked him out at the pound about eleven years ago. "He's mostly cocker spaniel," the people at the pound had said about the little black puppy. As it turned out, the only thing Bullwinkle had in common with a cocker spaniel was his thick black fur. When he's standing on his hind legs, he's taller than I am, and he weighs about one hundred thirty pounds. "Mostly Newfoundland" would have been closer to the truth.

For the party, Mom must have closed him up in the kitchen, because that's where the noise was coming from. Whenever Bullwinkle hears singing — or any kind of music — he howls his head off.

It was so piercing that some of the birthday guests actually covered their ears with their hands.

"George?" my mother called over the racket to my father, who was in the kitchen. "Would you please let the dog out into the backyard? I can't hear myself think!"

Let Bullwinkle out into the backyard? The four

of us stared at each other with just one thought in mind.

"Run for your lives!" I hissed.

But we weren't halfway to the gate when Bull-winkle galloped down the back steps looking for action, his fluffy tail waving in the air. When he gets out of the house, he usually circles the backyard a couple of times just to work off some energy.

That night, he started his circle, spotted us, and did a doggy double take. Then he charged after us like a stampeding buffalo!

Chapter
2

Patti has long legs — she's the tallest girl in our class. She made it to the gate first. She didn't even bother to open it — she climbed right over the top. The rest of us weren't so speedy.

Kate's a shorty and can't run very fast. I'm taller, and I was doing pretty well — dodging trees and bushes and lawn furniture — until I tripped over a sprinkler. I fell to my knees, and Kate and Stephanie fell on top of me. When we tried to stand up, Bullwinkle sideswiped us and knocked us down again.

"Sit, Bullwinkle! Stay!" I whispered sternly. *"Blech!"*

Bullwinkle was dragging his long, pink tongue across my face. I couldn't get up — one huge furry foot was pressed against my stomach, holding me down.

"Get him off!" I spluttered to Kate and Stephanie, just before Bullwinkle's tongue covered my face again like a damp washcloth.

"He's . . . he's eating the . . . the avocado mask!" Stephanie burst into giggles.

But she didn't think it was so funny when he started in on her — which Bullwinkle did as soon as he'd licked the last glob of green goop off *my* face.

"No, Bullwinkle! Stop that!" Stephanie shrieked.

"Sssh!" Kate and I hissed, both tugging at Bullwinkle's collar.

"I think somebody's coming!" Patti warned from the other side of the fence.

I looked over my shoulder. Someone was peering out the kitchen door!

"What's going on out there, Bullwinkle?" my father said. "Ann — where's the flashlight?" he called to my mother.

Bullwinkle trotted a few steps in the direction of the house — just long enough for Stephanie to scramble to her feet. Kate was already out the back gate. And I was right behind her — I made it just before Bullwinkle swung around. But I had to slam the gate closed in Stephanie's face!

"Are you crazy?" she panted. She was furious.

"Bullwinkle will get out!" I whispered. I didn't want to spend half the night chasing him around the neighborhood. "Climb over!"

I've never seen Stephanie move so fast! She was up and over the gate in a flash. She left a piece of her pajamas behind, however — a small, red-black-and-white tatter caught on the fence. Bullwinkle must have thought Stephanie left it for him, because he snatched it off the fence with his teeth.

"Your parents are standing on the back steps!" Kate whispered urgently.

She and Patti dashed down the alley and cut through the Fosters' yard. Stephanie and I were right behind them.

"Whew — safe! I don't think Mom and Dad saw us," I said as we crept past the Fosters'. We were at the far corner of the house when there was another pile-up!

"Watch it! You stepped right on my foot!" a squeaky voice complained.

"Melissa! What are you doing in the Fosters' yard?" Kate hissed.

"Tonight's our lucky night," Stephanie muttered to me.

14

"Oooowwww!" Melissa whined at her sister. "That hurt, Kate. I'm telling Mom you were running around outside in the dark . . . ooooo — what's that stuff on your face?!"

"You were spying on us, weren't you!" Kate growled. "And I've got news for you — you're outside in the dark, too." She made a grab for Melissa's ear, and Melissa shrieked.

"Somebody's going to hear!" I warned. "Let's get out of here!"

It was already too late. The third window from the end of the Fosters' house was raised with a screech, and a head appeared. "Hey, girls . . ." Donald Foster drawled. "What are you up to now?"

With a squeak, Melissa dashed through the hedge into the Beekmans' backyard. Patti jumped behind a bush. Between the avocado mask and the darkness, I couldn't be positive, but I just knew she was blushing.

"Is that you, Kate?" Donald shone his desk lamp out the window. "Wow — you look just like a movie star. You know the one I mean — the Slime Creature in *Curse of the Radioactive Swamp*?"

Kate's green mask did seem to glow a little. Stephanie snickered.

15

"Ha. Ha. Ha," Kate said coldly. "You're a laugh a minute, Donald." She marched around the house toward her own yard.

"And Lauren and Stephanie," Donald said, checking us out.

I was kind of glad Bullwinkle had taken care of *my* face.

"So that must be Patti behind the bush," Donald went on, aiming the lamp in Patti's direction for a second. "The Four Stooges."

"He thinks he's so cute!" I whispered indignantly to Stephanie.

"Well, he *is*!" she murmured back.

"So, Stephanie," Donald said suddenly, flashing her his smoothest grin. "I hear you're a pretty good dancer."

Out of the corner of my eye, I saw Patti sneaking across the yard after Kate.

"Well-l-l . . ." Stephanie was smiling modestly. She's very proud of her dancing — she's always picking up steps from rock videos and making up new ones herself.

"I'm not bad, either. You gonna dance with me at the Masons' party?"

"The Masons' party?" Stephanie and I looked at each other. It was the first we'd heard about it.

16

"I didn't know there was going to be a party at the Masons'," Stephanie said to Donald.

"When is it?" I asked.

"A dance, next Friday night," Donald said. "The invitations probably haven't been sent out yet — I know about the party because of Royce."

Royce Mason is a seventh-grader like Donald. He's got curly brown hair, big brown eyes, and a terrific smile. Kate has had a secret crush on him for months, since we watched him playing soccer after school. I'm the only one who knows about it, and I knew Kate would *die* when she heard about the party!

"Is it Royce's party?" I asked.

"Royce and Sally's," Donald answered. "I'm sure you're all invited."

Sally Mason is in our room, 5B, so we probably *were* all invited. Jenny Carlin's in 5B, too, and so is Pete Stone. Jenny just happens to like Pete, and, lately, Pete seems to like me. Which means Jenny doesn't like me much. If Sally asked everybody in our room, her party would be interesting.

"Kate's waiting for us," I said to Stephanie, who'd been hanging on Donald's every word. "Come on." I mean, we *were* in our pajamas, even if they were partly covered up.

"Oh. Yeah. See you, Donald." She gave him

her Brooke Shields smile, the one she practices in front of the mirror.

"Right — catch you at the party." Donald pulled down his window.

"Wow — a dance! Donald really is good-looking," Stephanie burbled as we crawled through the hedge.

"So he says." I've lived next door to Donald all my life, and I know just how boring he can be about himself.

Kate, Patti, and Melissa were standing on the Beekmans' back steps. "Can you believe what this twerp did?" Kate whispered when she saw us.

"Ow!" Melissa complained as Kate thumped her arm.

"What?" Stephanie asked.

"Pulled the door closed behind her when she left!"

"In other words . . ." I began.

"In other words . . . we're locked out!" Kate looked ready to throttle Melissa. "And don't you *dare* start crying!" she warned her little sister.

"What about climbing through a window?" Stephanie suggested.

Kate shook her head so hard that a big piece of dry avocado mask dropped off her chin. "Not unless we make a giant hole in a screen — Mom just had new catches put on all of them," she said gloomily. "I'll have to wake up my parents."

That wasn't the easiest thing, since the doorbell's really quiet, their bedroom is upstairs, and they'd already been asleep for a while. Kate called, then I did, until most of the dogs in the neighborhood were barking. It wasn't until Stephanie threw her sneaker at the upstairs window — Stephanie isn't much on sports, but she has a great throwing arm — that Mrs. Beekman finally woke up. And she wasn't at all happy about it.

"You girls," Mrs. Beekman groaned, letting us in the back door with a big yawn. "Kate, I've warned you about going outside at night."

"I told you so, Kate!" Melissa had to put in her two cents.

"You, too, young lady!" Mrs. Beekman said to Melissa. "Your father will talk to you both tomorrow."

"Great work!" Kate hissed at Melissa, who stuck out her tongue.

"It was my fault, Mrs. Beekman," Stephanie was confessing. "I just wanted to see a little of the surprise party at Lauren's. . . ."

"It's not a good idea to wander around the

neighborhood at eleven o'clock at night. Please go to bed, all of you — after you get that stuff off your faces."

We all crowded into the upstairs bathroom to wash our faces, although Bullwinkle had cleaned off Stephanie's and mine pretty thoroughly.

"What did you think of the mask?" Stephanie asked us when we were done. "Does your skin feel smooth? Tingly?"

"Well-l-l . . ." Patti touched her cheek and looked doubtful.

"Mine sure does," I said. "Bullwinkle gave my face a terrific massage."

Stephanie was looking in the mirror, practicing the Brooke Shields smile. She caught Kate's eye. "Do you think a seventh-grader could like a fifth-grader?"

Kate glanced quickly at me. I shook my head, meaning I hadn't opened my big mouth about her own crush on Royce. "Donald Foster," I explained.

"*Donald Foster?* Gross me out!" Kate made a gagging noise.

"I don't care what you say — *I* think he's cute," Stephanie replied. "And I'm going to dance with him as much as I can at the Masons' party. It would be cool to have a boyfriend who's older. . . ."

"The Masons' are having a party?" said Kate.

"Donald told us about it. It's going to be a dance party, and it's next Friday night — Sally and Royce together," I answered.

Kate nodded, looking pleased.

The Beekmans' portable television was in Kate's bedroom for the evening. Checking the TV listing, Stephanie announced, "There's something on Channel thirty-one called 'Beach Party Bongos' — anybody want to watch it?"

"I've had enough parties for one night, thank you," Kate said.

As we flopped down on Kate's big bed, Patti added, "At least there's one thing to be grateful for."

"Like what?" I asked.

"Like the fact that we didn't have that honey conditioner on our hair. By the time Bullwinkle finished with us, we might all have been bald!"

Chapter 3

We were sitting at the breakfast table the next morning, working on our second helpings of blueberry waffles, when the mail arrived at the Beekmans'.

"Junk, bill, junk, bill, bill," Mrs. Beekman muttered as she sorted it out. "Kate, here's something for you."

"It looks like an invitation!" Stephanie exclaimed as Kate tore open the small red envelope.

"It is!" Kate held the card up for us to see. On the front it had a boy and girl dancing, with a bunch of balloons floating over their heads. Then she read the inside: "Royce and Sally Mason are having a party. It's next Friday night at seven-thirty. Casual."

"I wonder if we all got one," I said.

"You think Sally would ask one of us and not the rest, when she knows we're best friends?" Kate shook her head.

"I'm going to need a whole new look," Stephanie said thoughtfully.

"I'd like to find some yellow sneakers. Maybe we should go to the mall this afternoon," Kate suggested.

"Oh," I said. I glanced at Patti and Stephanie. We'd already made secret plans to shop for Kate's birthday present that day.

"Er . . ." Patti said. She blushed bright red.

"I really can't," Stephanie said quickly. "I've got a . . . a . . . hair appointment at Cut-Ups."

"You're having your hair cut?" Kate said, surprised. Stephanie's hair is dark, wavy, and *very* long — she hasn't had it cut since second grade.

"Uh . . . I've been thinking about it for a while," Stephanie said, ducking the question.

Kate turned to Patti and me. "What about you two?"

Thanks to Stephanie, we'd had time to think of excuses.

"I have to baby-sit Harold," Patti said. Harold is Patti's little brother.

"I told Mom I'd go with her to visit Aunt Beth," I said.

"Kate, talk to your father before you make plans to go anywhere," Mrs. Beekman said from the living room. "I'm not happy about last night."

"We could shop Monday after school," I suggested.

"Good idea," Stephanie said.

Patti nodded in agreement.

"Okay — Monday after school we'll do the mall," Kate said.

Stephanie checked her watch. "I guess I'd better get home. I have stuff to do around the house." She carried her breakfast dishes over to the dishwasher.

"Me, too." I stood up, and so did Patti.

"Good-bye, Mrs. Beekman. And about last night —" Stephanie said.

"We won't do it again," I said.

"And thank you for the breakfast," Patti added.

Mrs. Beekman waved from behind her newspaper.

Stephanie and Patti retrieved their bikes from the Beekmans' garage. Kate and I walked down the driveway with them.

Kate stopped at the street. "I'll talk to you later — I'd better go face Dad."

"Good luck."

I turned up the sidewalk toward my house.

"I'll call you as soon as I get home!" Stephanie hissed as she and Patti pedaled past.

"Don't slam it!" my mother whispered as I walked through our front door. "Your brother is still asleep."

"Was Linda's party okay?" I asked innocently, picking up the mail from the table in the hall.

Mom nodded. "She was really surprised, and everybody seemed to have a good time." Mom went on, "We had to put Bullwinkle outside, and he acted a little odd. . . ."

"Oh, really?" I sifted through the magazines and newspapers. Poor Bullwinkle — Mom thought he was acting wacko all by himself, when really we had gotten him crazy, sneaking around with tasty green faces. "He's getting kind of old and silly."

"Yes," my mother said, "he came back inside chewing a piece of red, black, and white striped cloth. The colors made me think of Stephanie. . . ." She gave me the once-over.

I pulled a small red envelope out of the stack of mail. "The invitation!" Then the telephone rang and I ran for it.

"It's me," Stephanie said. "Did you get one?"

25

"Yeah."

"Me, too, and so did Patti. I can't wait! Now — what about this afternoon? Where do you want to meet?"

"What about in front of Dandelion?"

Dandelion's a store on Main Street that sells great kids' clothes.

"Okay — we'll probably find the perfect present right there. I'll tell Patti we'll be waiting out front."

"Do you still think Kate's party ought to be a surprise?" I asked. "Last night she sure sounded as though she doesn't like surprise parties."

"Oh, everybody says that," Stephanie replied breezily. "But when it happens to *you*, you love it! Are you kidding me — who doesn't like being the absolute center of attention?"

"Well . . . maybe." Stephanie might, but would Kate?

"Besides, after all that stuff she said about any jerk being able to figure it out, it's a challenge! I want to see her face when we yell 'surprise!' " Stephanie said gleefully. "So what about this afternoon — is two o'clock all right?"

"Sure," I said.

"Two o'clock in front of Dandelion. See you."

I was a little late getting there. By the time I rode

up on my bike, Stephanie and Patti were already window-shopping.

"What about that orange T-shirt?" Patti was saying.

"On Kate? I wouldn't like the color on her," Stephanie answered.

"Hi, guys," I said. "See anything?"

"Not out here," Stephanie answered. "Let's go inside."

Instead of getting Kate three little presents this year, we'd decided to buy her one big present from all three of us. "Something super special," Stephanie had said.

But that meant finding one thing we all agreed on. And that wasn't so easy, not even at Dandelion.

"This is sharp," Stephanie said, unfolding a long red sweat shirt silk-screened with black and white palm trees.

I never even thought about red, white, and black clothes until I met Stephanie. But she manages to find them everywhere. "That looks exactly like *you*, Stephanie. Not like Kate," I said.

"What about these?" Patti held up some baggy gray denim pants.

"I like them," I said.

"Not zippy enough," said Stephanie.

"We know she wants yellow sneakers." Patti picked up a pair with bright green laces.

Stephanie and I both shook our heads. "What's the fun in giving her something she needs?" Stephanie said. "The present — and the party — have to be real surprises."

"It's a good thing we've started looking two weeks ahead of time," I told them. "I have a feeling we'll need at least that long to find something we all like."

After we looked at every single item in Dandelion, Stephanie said, "We'd better try the mall — there's always Just Juniors."

"And Kid Works," Patti added. "We're bound to turn up something at one of them."

But we went through all the shelves and racks in both stores and didn't find anything right for Kate.

"I don't know. . . ." Stephanie took a last look around Kid Works. "I do kind of like the blue skirt."

"Can you seriously picture Kate in an electric-blue satin mini?" I asked Patti. Kate's idea of far-out clothes is a checkered shirt with striped pants, in matching colors.

Patti giggled and shook her head.

"I'm starving," I said then. "Let's go to Sweet Stuff."

Sweet Stuff has the best chocolate candy in Riverhurst. I bought a small bag of caramels, Patti got some white chocolate bark, and Stephanie picked a bag of chocolate-covered almonds.

We walked around until we found an empty bench and sat down.

"If I gain weight in my face, it's your fault, Lauren." Stephanie sucked her cheeks in, then popped two almonds into her mouth. "We hardly ever come to this end of the mall," she said, looking around.

"There's nothing much down here," I said. "A store that sells sheets and towels, one for pool equipment, an auto supply place. . . ."

"Isn't that a pet shop?" Patti asked.

"I never noticed it before — it must be new," I said, strolling toward it.

The store had two big windows in front. A small sign hung in one of them: Pets of Distinction. Beneath it, three white poodle puppies raced around in the cedar shavings.

"Look — kittens!" Stephanie cried.

In the other window, a crowd of kittens climbed and leaped and stalked — long-haired, short-haired, in every color from black to orange to gray.

"Aren't they cute? I love the one with black-and-white spots!" said Stephanie.

"Oh, look at the little gray one!" Patti tapped

the glass at a plump gray kitten with white feet and big blue eyes.

"Hey — a calico! That's it!" I exclaimed.

"What's it?" said Stephanie.

"The perfect birthday present for Kate!" I said. "A calico kitten!"

The calico was curled in a big fluffy ball next to the water dish, sound asleep. It was a mixture of colors: orange, white, and black. A huge, feathery tail lay over its round side.

"You think so? Does Kate even like pets?" Patti wanted to know.

"She's never had any, has she?" Stephanie asked.

"Maybe her parents don't like them," Patti said. "Mine don't."

"Kate had a cat before you knew her," I told Stephanie. "It died when we were in the third grade. The cat's name was Batik, and she was a big, fat calico. Kate just loved Batik, and so did her parents — it was *their* cat before Kate was even born."

"Then why didn't they get another one?" Stephanie asked.

"I guess they were too upset at first," I replied. "And they had Melissa to deal with. . . ."

Stephanie nodded. "Melissa's a full-time job."

30

She opened the door of Pets of Distinction. "Let's go in."

"Shouldn't we check with Mrs. Beekman to see if it's okay?" Patti asked.

"First let's check out the calico."

Chapter
4

"May I help you, girls?" A woman in a light-blue sweater popped out from behind a row of bird cages. "Perhaps you'd like a parakeet? Or maybe a long-haired guinea pig? Easy to take care of, and they're great pets."

"No, thank you," Stephanie said. "We're interested in one of the kittens in the front window."

The woman clapped her hands together. "Aren't they dear?" she trilled. She steered us over to the window and opened a wire gate. "Which kitten did you have in mind?"

"The calico," I answered. "Next to the water dish."

"You certainly have an eye for special cats," the woman said.

She picked up the sleepy kitten and handed it to me. It yawned, showing its sharp little teeth and rough pink tongue. Then it mewed at me. It was darling!

Patti stroked the kitten's head. "It's so soft — like a cotton ball."

"*She*," the woman corrected. "All tricolored cats are females. She has long, soft hair because her mother is a purebred Persian."

"Wow! Is she expensive?" I asked, touching the kitten's pink nose.

"Only forty dollars," the woman said.

"Oh. Thank you," I said. *But no thanks* — I handed the kitten right back. We had each planned to spend around six or seven dollars on Kate's present. I didn't know about Stephanie, or Patti, but I didn't have a dime extra.

"Perhaps you'd like to consider one of the other kittens," the woman suggested. "The black-and-white kitten and the gray one are twenty-five dollars each."

"No — we really wanted a calico," I said, discouraged. "Thanks very much."

After we'd left the store, we stopped in front of the window to take another look at the kittens. "It's too bad she costs so much," I said, watching the calico chasing her long, fluffy tail. "Kate would have just loved her."

"We only need around twenty dollars more," Stephanie said. "The three of us could probably make that much."

"That's right!" Patti agreed. "We could run errands for people in the neighborhood. . . ."

"Or rake leaves . . ." I added, getting into the spirit.

"Wash cars — my dad's car needs washing. We've got a couple of weeks to make the money," Stephanie pointed out. "We'll come back and buy the kitten."

"But what if somebody else buys her first?" I said.

"Spend forty dollars on a kitten? We're the only ones crazy enough to do that!" Stephanie replied with a grin. "Let's go to my house and think of more things we could do to make money."

We were on our way across the mall, headed for the rack where we'd left our bikes . . . when we ran right smack into Kate Beekman!

"Yikes!" I murmured.

"Kate!" Stephanie practically shrieked. "What are you doing here?! I thought your dad would make you stay in."

"Dad just gave me a warning," Kate replied. "What about you? I thought you were all too busy to come to the mall this afternoon." She was frowning.

I didn't want Kate to think we were sneaking around to have fun without her. It would be better to tell her about the surprise party than to hurt her feelings.

"Actually, Kate," I began, "we were. . . ."

But I hadn't counted on Stephanie. "Actually, Kate, we were on our way to Cut-Ups," she broke in, shooting me a stern look. "Patti doesn't have to baby-sit until later, so she said she'd come with me. We detoured through the mall" — Stephanie ran out of inspiration for a split second, but she got going again fast — "where we ran into Lauren, who's here because . . ."

Everybody looked at me, waiting for an explanation.

"Because Mom and Aunt Beth wanted to buy some sheets and towels. They're trotting around here someplace," I said, waving in the direction of the towel store.

"And . . . uh . . . Lauren decided to come with us to Cut-Ups," Patti finished.

"Hmmm." Would Kate go for the story? "In that

35

case," she said, "I'll come, too. Stephanie getting a haircut is a big event."

Stephanie, Patti, and I stared at each other. The whole story was made up. We would arrive at Cut-Ups and of course Stephanie wouldn't have an appointment. But what else could we do?

"Great!" said Stephanie brightly.

We marched through the mall to the other entrance, crossed two parking lots, and walked into Cut-Ups. Just inside the door was an old juke box, the kind with big tubes of colored lights running up the sides.

"Neat!" Kate said. She and Patti stopped to see what records it played.

Stephanie and I went to the big round desk, where a thin man with a flat-top haircut was sitting.

"My name is Stephanie Green," Stephanie said in a low voice. "I don't have an appointment. I don't suppose you could — "

"Oh, my! Elaine Green's little girl? Elaine is one of my favorite customers." The man talked a mile a minute. "I'm Larry," he said, shaking hands with both of us. "I own this place. Stephanie, Elaine is so proud of you. I've seen hundreds of pictures of you — I'd recognize you anywhere."

He looked at the big appointment book on the

desk in front of him. "And of course I'll fit you in. Please take a seat — I promise it won't be *too* long."

"Thank you," Stephanie said, smiling stiffly. "I didn't want to be fitted in!" she whispered to me. "And how am I supposed to pay for this?"

"Tell Kate what we're up to, and forget the whole thing," I suggested.

"No way! Kate is going to be surprised, all right!"

"You know how you were talking about a new look?" I reminded her. "I think you're about to get one."

Larry was as good as his word. We sat down to read the fashion magazines that were lying around the salon. We hadn't been there more than ten minutes when Larry called out, "Stephanie — I can style you now!"

"Coming . . ." Stephanie groaned. It took her about a minute to go ten steps. It was like she was walking to her doom.

Stephanie lowered herself into the chair.

"We'll wash your hair first," Larry said.

"I just washed it a few hours ago," Stephanie told him.

"Then we'll wet it down," said Larry, grabbing a spray bottle, "and jump right in."

Stephanie nodded, too uneasy to practice her smile in the mirror in front of her.

Larry held up a strand of Stephanie's hair that looked about three feet long. "How much do you want me to take off?" he asked her.

"Uh — I guess I just want a trim," Stephanie said nervously.

"How about if I get rid of the split ends, and then we'll see?" Larry suggested.

"Okay." Stephanie closed her eyes tight as Larry picked up the scissors.

The rest of us wouldn't have missed it for the world.

"I can't believe she's doing this," Kate murmured.

"Neither can I," I said.

And if Kate had known the reason why, she'd have been even more amazed: Stephanie would rather get her hair cut than give in and tell Kate about the surprise party!

Snip — a handful of Stephanie's hair fell to the floor.

Stephanie moaned softly.

Snip — another handful. *Snip, snip* — pretty soon the floor around the chair was absolutely covered with dark, wavy hair.

"Hey," I said. "It's starting to look good!"

"It is?" Stephanie opened one eye, slowly. Then she opened the other. She looked hard at herself in the mirror and sucked in her cheeks. "I think it makes my face look thinner!" she exclaimed. "Larry, let's go for it!"

When Larry finally put down his scissors, Stephanie had short curls all around her face and loose waves to her shoulders on the sides and in the back.

"You look terrific!" Patti, Kate, and I declared.

"She looks like an *angel*," said Larry, twisting the short curls around the end of his comb for the finishing touch.

Stephanie climbed down from the chair. "I'll pay and meet you outside," she said to us.

She seemed pretty gloomy as the four of us walked back to the mall together.

"Your hair really does look fabulous," I told her.

"Yeah, but I had to give Larry the birthday money and everything else I had in my wallet, and Mom still owes him twenty dollars," Stephanie told me under her breath.

"Will you have to pay your mom back?" I asked.

"No — she'll be ecstatic that I finally got a hair cut," Stephanie said. "But now we have even more money to make before we can buy the calico."

Almost thirty dollars in two weeks. Could we do it?

Chapter
5

Patti, Stephanie, and I had promised to go shopping with Kate on Monday afternoon, but that was definitely out now. We had a job washing Stephanie's father's car, and we couldn't afford to pass it up.

Kate had been half-asleep on the way to school that morning, so she hadn't remembered to ask us about going to the mall. But I knew she would at lunch.

"We'll have to come up with more excuses," I murmured to Stephanie in the lunch line at the school cafeteria.

"I love your hair, Stephanie," Tracy Osner called out as she carried her tray into the lunch room.

"Thanks, Tracy," Stephanie said. "I've already

thought of my excuse," she went on in a lower voice. "I'm going to say my grandmother's coming out from the city for a visit, and I have to stay at home."

Sure enough, Kate mentioned the mall as soon as we'd sat down at our regular table. Stephanie explained about her grandmother's visit. Patti said she had to take care of Harold again, because both of her parents were giving exams that afternoon. Patti's parents are professors at the university.

"Then I guess it's just you and me, Lauren," Kate said.

"Oh, Kate — I can't." I used at least a small particle of truth in my story. "Mom found out about us sneaking around on Friday night from Bullwinkle. . . ."

"Bullwinkle?" Stephanie burst out. She obviously thought I'd flipped!

"Bullwinkle," I repeated firmly. "He had a scrap of *your* pajamas in his mouth when he trotted back inside our house. Red, black, and white striped? Mom put two and two together, and — "

"And came up with the four of us." Stephanie nodded.

"So Dad grounded me until Wednesday," I said to Kate.

Kate looked really disappointed.

42

"I'm sorry." I felt awful, lying to my best friend.

"That's all right," Kate said.

But it's no fun, going shopping alone.

"This will be a lot harder for me to manage than it will be for you," I pointed out to Stephanie and Patti that afternoon. "Stephanie, you're at the opposite end of Pine Street, and Patti's in a completely different neighborhood. But Kate and I practically live in each other's houses. I don't know how I can keep this up for two weeks without her catching on."

"Maybe Stephanie and I can take some jobs without you," Patti suggested. "And you can do something with Kate."

"Right — kind of throw her off the trail," Stephanie said. "It might work. Lauren, pass me the sponge."

We were washing Stephanie's father's car in the Greens' driveway.

"That doesn't seem fair to you two," I said, turning the hose on the back bumper of the car. "Maybe we should just tell Kate about the present and the party. It would make things a lot easier."

"But do you think Kate would let us keep on working if she knew we were doing it just to buy her a birthday present?" Patti asked.

"Of course not," Stephanie said.

43

They were right — Kate would be embarrassed by all the fuss.

"There you are," Stephanie said, giving the headlights a swipe. "So the calico kitten's still a surprise, and the party's still a surprise. Patti, please throw some of that soapy water on the windshield."

We made seven dollars and fifty cents washing the car on Monday, and ten dollars repainting Patti's mother's gardening shed on Tuesday. We were getting there!

That night, my mom called Mrs. Beekman for me — just in case Kate answered the phone. Then she put me on.

"Hi, Mrs. Beekman," I said.

"Hi, Lauren," Mrs. Beekman whispered. "Kate's in the kitchen. Is there some problem with you girls? You haven't been around much recently."

"We're planning a party for Kate's birthday," I told her. "And we're trying to keep it a surprise."

"What a nice idea." Mrs. Beekman sounded relieved. "Is there anything I can do to help?"

"Actually, I wanted to ask you about the present. We'd like to get her a kitten," I said. "A calico kitten."

Mrs. Beekman was quiet for a moment. "How

lovely. I can't imagine anything that Kate would like more."

"Terrific! We've found the cutest one at — "

"That's right, Mr. Tully," Mrs. Beekman said suddenly. Kate must have walked into the room. "Two pounds of swordfish steaks, and I'll pick them up tomorrow. Thank you."

"Thank *you*, Mrs. Beekman." I hung up. It was okay! Things were going great!

But on Wednesday, our luck changed.

Mom had run into Mrs. Carter earlier that week in town. Mrs. Carter is very old — she taught Mom in elementary school — and very crotchety. She wondered if Roger would be interested in spending Wednesday afternoon cleaning up her yard. She'd be willing to pay him fifteen dollars, she said.

Roger turned the offer down flat. "Mrs. Carter always makes me feel as though I'm back in the second grade."

So Mom suggested Stephanie, Patti, and me. And Mrs. Carter agreed to try us out.

"On the minus side, Mrs. Carter is super cranky," I told Stephanie and Patti. "And she lives only a street away from Kate and me, which means Kate might spot us."

45

"Not necessarily," Stephanie argued. "And on the plus side, fifteen more dollars would buy the calico kitten *this week*, with two-fifty left over for Sweet Stuff."

So Wednesday afternoon found the three of us lined up in Mrs. Carter's garage. Mrs. Carter looks sort of like a witch, with a long, thin nose and flyaway white hair.

As she handed out the tools, she gave us instructions in a high, scratchy voice: "Don't step in the flower beds while you're weeding. In tight spots, always weed by hand — don't use the hoe, because you'll tear everything up. Pick the leaves out of the borders — don't rake them. Don't scratch the trunks of my fruit trees with the rake. Break twigs up into small pieces before you pile them — neatly! — in the trash bin." And on and on.

"I didn't think we were ever going to get started," Patti said to Stephanie and me as we shouldered our rakes and walked onto the lawn.

"And don't spend all your time chatting!" Mrs. Carter screeched from the house. "I've hired you to *work* in my garden!"

"Ugh! If I'd had her for a teacher, I definitely would have been a second-grade dropout!" Stephanie muttered.

46

"Raking will be a breeze, compared to listening to Mrs. Carter," I said.

But we hadn't been raking more than a few minutes when Patti said, "Oh, no! Kate's coming around the corner on her bike!"

"Hide!" Stephanie squawked.

But where? We couldn't step in the flower beds, and there were little fences around most of the trees, and Mrs. Carter had closed the garage doors. So we just stood there, holding our rakes, looking dumb.

Kate braked her bike in a cloud of dust and stared at us. Finally she spoke. "I called your houses — I wondered where you all were. What are you doing in Mrs. Carter's yard?"

"We needed a little extra money," Stephanie said. "I had to pay Mom back for my haircut."

"I owed Roger," I said.

"I owed Harold," said Patti. That wasn't as silly as it sounded. Harold is only six, but he has a lot of money in his bear bank because he never spends a cent.

"Oh," said Kate. "Why didn't you tell me about it?"

"It was a spur-of-the-moment kind of thing," Stephanie replied.

"I did call, but no one answered," I lied.

47

"Oh," Kate said again. "I must have been outside." But I knew she didn't believe me.

Mrs. Carter bolted out of her house about then. "Girls," she yelled, "this is not a party! Do you hear me?"

"You bet it isn't!" mumbled Stephanie.

"I'd better go." Kate climbed back on her bike.

"Kate — wait!" I called. But Kate was already halfway down the street.

The four of us met at the corner, as usual, the next morning to ride to school together on our bicycles. But Kate was awfully quiet. She didn't say much at lunch, either. When she asked if we were busy that afternoon, and we said yes, she didn't even try to find out what we were doing.

We were going to the mall to buy the kitten, of course. On the way over I said, "I'm worried about Kate. What good is surprising her with a birthday party, if we're losing her as a friend?"

"You're letting your imagination run away with you, Lauren," Stephanie said.

That's something Kate always says to me. Having Stephanie say it just made me feel worse about Kate.

"Look — we're going to buy the kitten right now.

Once we have the present, things will get back to normal," Stephanie promised.

We dashed across the mall, past auto supplies and dishes, to Pets of Distinction.

"The calico kitten isn't in the window!" Patti exclaimed.

"The black-and-white spotted one isn't here, either," Stephanie said. "They're probably in a cage inside."

We pushed open the door and hurried into the store.

"We were in here on Saturday," I said to the woman in the blue sweater. "We were interested in the calico kitten — the one that cost forty dollars?"

"Oh, isn't that a shame!" the woman said. "I sold the kitten not two hours ago to a little boy and his mother."

So it was back to square one. We were so depressed that we passed right by Sweet Stuff without a second glance.

Chapter 6

It was my turn to have the sleepover on Friday. Stephanie, Patti, and Kate would bring their overnight stuff to my house. Then my parents would drive us to the Masons' party and pick us up when it was over.

Kate is always on time, but she wasn't that night. It gave Patti, Stephanie, and me a chance to discuss the problem of the present with my mother. When Kate finally knocked, she was twenty minutes late — and she only lives two minutes away at the most.

Another thing — the Sleepover Friends had decided early in the week what to wear to the party. We'd all agreed on pants with the cuffs rolled up, two shirts, and colored sneaks. Kate walked in the front door wearing a long printed sweater, pink leggings, and gray high-tops.

"Whoa!" said Stephanie.

Kate's blonde hair is short and neat. She usually brushes it away from her face and forgets about it. Now it was pulled straight back on one side with a red plastic clip. And she was wearing earrings — long, dangly, clip-on e*arrings*!

Kate looked at each one of us, as though she just dared us to say something.

"I like your earrings, Kate," Patti said quietly.

"Thanks. They're not really mine — they belong to Tracy Osner," Kate said coolly. "The hair clip is Jenny's."

"Jenny's?" said Stephanie.

"Jenny Carlin," Kate replied. "Since you were all busy, I rode home with Tracy and Jenny after school yesterday."

Tracy's okay, but Jenny Carlin? I couldn't believe what I was hearing. I can't stand Jenny Carlin, and Kate very well knows it.

"We're ready to go, aren't we?" Patti asked in the nick of time.

"More than ready," my mother said. "Kate, did you forget your pajamas?"

51

Kate never forgets anything. "I'll pick them up later," she answered vaguely.

We climbed into the car — Stephanie, Patti, and I in the back seat, Kate up front with my mom.

The ride over was so quiet that I could hear Kate's watch ticking. Nobody said a thing — and I forgot to breathe a couple of times. When my mother pulled up in front of the Masons', Kate was the first person out of the car and into the house.

"Oh, dear," Mom said. "Don't you think you should tell Kate about her party?"

"We'd like it to be a surprise, Mrs. Hunter," Stephanie replied firmly.

"Well . . . try to have a good time at the dance. Lauren's dad will be back for you at ten, girls."

Inside, there were balloons and colored lights and streamers and music: Sally and Royce's older sister was playing the tapes for dancing. There must have been at least forty people at the party: a bunch of fifth-graders, some sixth-graders, lots of Royce's seventh-grade friends. Half of the kids were already jumping around to the music.

I saw Larry Jackson and Henry Larkin and some other kids from our room, 5B, but Kate had disappeared.

Michael Pastore, a fifth-grader in the A room, asked Patti to dance. He really likes her, even though he's shorter than she is. She hunched down and looked uncomfortable. But the height difference didn't seem to bother Michael at all.

"Hi, Lauren." It was Pete Stone in a really great checkered sweatshirt. "Want to get something to eat?"

Mrs. Mason was behind the refreshment table. She's one of the class mothers who helps out on field trips and at book fairs and stuff. She's a nice person, but very nervous. And she's just as nervous in her own house as she is when she's with us at the zoo or the museum.

Mrs. Mason has a choppy way of talking. She's also into health food. "Lauren. Good evening. Nice to see you. And Pete. What would. You like? The whole-grain bread. Is. Good. Yogurt dip? With celery sticks?"

"Hello, Mrs. Mason. Just some punch would be fine."

It tasted like carrots, but Pete and I both drank a cup. That's when I saw Kate. She was standing with Tracy Osner and Jenny Carlin . . . and they were all dressed alike! Jenny was wearing red leggings, and Tracy wore blue ones. Both of them had clips in their hair and earrings dangling from their ears!

Tracy waved, but Jenny glared at Pete and me. Kate stared right past us.

I danced with Pete and Larry and Michael. Patti danced with Michael, and with Kyle Hubbard, another boy in 5A, and a tall sixth-grader named Ricky Delman. Stephanie danced with Larry, two sixth-graders, and Donald Foster — three times. Kate even danced with Royce Mason twice.

But I was too worried to really have fun. "Tonight at the sleepover," I said to Stephanie and Patti, "I'm going to tell Kate everything."

"I think we should," Patti agreed.

Even Stephanie finally admitted things had gone too far.

But Kate wouldn't let me tell her. When Dad stopped the car in our driveway after the party, Kate said, "Goodnight, Mr. Hunter. Thank you for the ride." Then she got out and walked quickly down the sidewalk toward her house. She wasn't going for her pajamas — she wasn't coming to my sleepover!

"Hey, wait a second!" I got out of the car and ran down the sidewalk after her. "I have something to tell you!"

Kate whirled around. "I don't want to hear it, Lauren Hunter!" she snapped. "I never thought I'd be saying this, but Jenny Carlin is acting more like a friend than you are. You and Stephanie and Patti don't do anything with me anymore. You've lied to me. You've probably even told them about me and Royce Mason, so you can laugh about it!"

I was shocked! "Kate, you asked me to keep it a secret — I would never tell anyone. You're my best friend!"

"You have a pretty weird way of showing it, Lauren! I don't think you care about me at all!"

"Listen to me! The reason we've — "

"Forget it! You're too late!" She turned on her heel and marched away.

Stephanie and Patti raced up behind me.

"Isn't she coming back?" Patti asked.

I shook my head. "She's furious. What a mess!" I opened the back door. "And I'm absolutely starving."

I'm lucky I come from a thin family because I like to eat. I eat quite a lot when I'm happy. But when I'm upset, I can eat twice as much. And I was upset that night — it was the very first sleepover in our history without Kate.

I started stirring up things in the kitchen: two big bowls of caramel popcorn, Dr. Pepper floats for the three of us, plates of nachos made with corn chips and melted cheese with an olive on top, chocolate-chip refrigerator cookies. We piled everything on a tray, and I carried it upstairs to my room.

"Where's Bullwinkle?" Stephanie asked.

"Locked in the spare room," I replied.

"Just checking."

"What are we going to do about Kate?" Patti asked.

"We have to do *something*, quick. If Lauren keeps feeding me like this, I'm going to be sick, *plus* gain a few hundred pounds," Stephanie said. She ate three more nachos.

Chapter
7

When we got up the next morning, my father was sitting at the breakfast table alone. "Something to eat, ladies?" he asked.

Stephanie clutched her stomach and groaned. "No, thanks, Mr. Hunter. I don't think I'll ever eat again."

Patti shook her head, too. "I'll just have some ice water."

I wasn't even hungry. That Friday night had been the pig-out of all time. I was amazed that there was anything left in the refrigerator for Dad to be eating.

"Where's Mom?" I asked.

"She had an important errand to run," he answered. "She told me to tell you three not to leave the house before she gets back."

"Oh?" We hadn't done anything to get into trouble. I wondered what Mom wanted.

We didn't have to wait long to find out. I heard Mom's car pull up in the driveway. Then she nudged the back door once or twice. I ran to open it. Mom was carrying a cardboard box so large that I could only see her legs.

"I think I've solved one of your big problems — although I've given myself a few new little ones," she announced from behind the box.

Something inside the box thumped and bumped . . . and squeaked!

"What's in there, Mrs. Hunter?" Stephanie asked as Mom set the box down on the kitchen floor.

"Take a look," Mom said, opening the top flaps.

Stephanie, Patti, and I peered inside. The box was a mass of wriggling, scrambling, squirming . . .

"Wow — a boxful of kittens!" I exclaimed.

"Well, really only four," my mother said.

"And one's a calico!" said Stephanie.

Half the kitten's face was black, the other half orange. She had a white chin and stomach, four little white paws, and a mischievous expression in her clear green eyes.

Besides the calico, there were two black-and-white kittens and a solid black one in the box.

"Oh, Mom — where did you find them?"

"An advertisement in this morning's paper — 'free kittens to good homes.' Since the ad listed a calico, I thought I'd take a look."

"What about the other three, Mrs. Hunter?" Patti asked.

"The owner was all set to take them to the pound," my mother said. "I couldn't let that happen, could I? I figured we could find somebody to adopt them."

"Mom, you're great!" I gave her a hug. "Now we have Kate's present — and exactly a week to get her to talk to us."

"Why should we wait a week for her birthday? I think the surprise party should be *today*," Stephanie declared.

"You're kidding!" I said. "Kate probably won't even let us *near* her house!"

"She may not let *us* in, but she's not going to stop a delivery man, is she?" Stephanie replied craftily.

"What kind of delivery man?" Patti asked.

"Oh — I think we'll start with a heart-shaped pizza for twelve from Pizza Dreams — triples for each of us. And then an ice-cream cake shaped like a cat from Russells'. And maybe a singing telegram from Sneak Attack. Thanks to Lauren's mom, we've got forty-two fifty to spend, remember?"

"Balloons would be nice," I said thoughtfully.

"Balloons *would* be nice," Stephanie agreed.

"With 'Happy Birthday' on them, and lots of ribbons," Patti added.

"I think we might be able to slip in with the balloons," I said.

"When is all this going to start?" my mother asked, smiling at us.

"Around four this afternoon," Stephanie said.

"Then I'd better warn Barbara Beekman," Mom said, picking up the telephone.

"But tell her it's still a secret, Mom," I cautioned.

"Oh, yes — I'll tell her that," my mother said.

Patti and I reached into the cardboard box to pick up the kittens, but Stephanie shook her head. "No time for that now," she scolded. "We have to get all of this coordinated."

She and Patti called home to get permission to stay at my house for the day. Then we worked out a timetable on a sheet of paper.

"Four o'clock — the singing telegram," Stephanie began.

"Okay." I wrote it down. "Four-fifteen — the pizza."

"No," said Patti. "I think the ice-cream cake should be delivered first because it can be put in the freezer. The pizza would get cold waiting for the ice-cream cake, and then us, to show up."

"You're right. Ice-cream cake at four-fifteen. Pizza at four-thirty. Then us, with the balloons and the kitten, at four-thirty-two."

"When Kate sees the kitten, she'll have to let us in," Patti said, bending over to pat the calico.

We rode our bikes to Pizza Dreams, and Russells', and Sneak Attack. After we'd paid for the pizza, the ice-cream cake, and the singing telegram — to be performed by a clown — we had thirteen dollars and fifty cents left.

"This should buy plenty of balloons," Stephanie said. "Let's go to Looney Balloons at the mall."

The guys there blew up fifteen enormous red helium balloons with HAPPY BIRTHDAY stamped on them in silver glitter. They fastened them with crinkly silver and red ribbon. Just looking at the balloons could put you in a good mood.

We tied them to our bikes, five balloons each, and rode slowly home. We turned up the alley behind my house, so Kate wouldn't see them before we wanted her to.

My room has a good view of Kate's front yard. We carried the kittens upstairs and took turns keeping watch out the window.

It was Stephanie who spotted the truck from Sneak Attack. "He's here — four o'clock, on the dot!"

Patti and I ran to the window.

"What's he wearing?"

"A white jacket with red pom-poms for buttons . . ."

"An orange wig, striped trousers . . ."

"Big red lips and a rubber nose . . ."

"Look at his *feet!*"

The clown stepped out of the truck onto the ground in shoes that looked four feet long.

"His feet are bigger than Robert Ellwanger's," Stephanie snickered — Robert Ellwanger is the nerdiest boy in Riverhurst.

The clown reached back into the truck for a large drum with a horn attached. Then he stumbled up the walk to the Beekmans' front door. He rang the door bell.

In a few seconds, someone opened the door.

"It's Kate!" Stephanie hissed.

The clown asked her a question. Kate nodded.

The clown took a step back. Then he started banging on the drum, tooting the horn, and singing "Happy Birthday to You" in between toots.

"That's the funniest thing I've ever seen!" I giggled.

"He's totally off-key!" Stephanie shrieked, falling onto the bed. "What's Kate doing?"

There was a mournful howl from Bullwinkle in the backyard.

"Kate's starting to laugh," Patti said. "Watch it — she's looking this way!"

Things moved pretty quickly after that. Fifteen minutes later, the van from Russells' drove to the Beekmans' house. A man in a blue uniform got out, carrying a big blue-and-white box. He rang the doorbell, and Kate opened the door. After a word or two, he handed Kate the box, bowed deeply, and went back to his truck.

"We'd better get ready," Patti advised. "It's pizza next, and then we're on."

We put the two black-and-whites and the solid black kitten back in their box in the kitchen. Patti carried the little calico into the living room, where we'd left the balloons.

They were bumping against the ceiling, their silver and red ribbons hanging down to the floor. I grabbed the ribbons to five of the balloons and handed them to Stephanie.

"You take five . . . no, maybe you should take more. If Patti carries the kitten, she can't hold any balloons."

"What if we hooked one balloon to the kitten?" Stephanie suggested. "It would look really cute."

Patti nodded.

"Okay." I wrapped some ribbon loosely around the kitten's neck, and handed the end closest to the balloon to Patti to hang on to. Stephanie had seven balloons, I had seven, and Patti had one, plus the kitten. We were all set.

"I hear a truck!" Stephanie said.

I peeked through the curtains. "Pizza Dreams! Let's go!"

I opened the front door and we squeezed through it — the balloons were really big. We started down the sidewalk looking a little like a circus parade, with lots of balloons and one small animal.

We were almost to Kate's house when I heard a commotion behind us — kind of a huffing and grunting and scrabbling.

Patti looked back. "It's Bullwinkle!" she screamed.

Somehow he had heaved himself over the fence and was heading right for us!

The pizza man practically dumped the pizza on Kate and dashed for his truck. But Bullwinkle was interested only in the balloons!

"He thinks they're gigantic rubber balls," I panted to Stephanie and Patti as we ducked and dodged out of his way.

Kate was on her front steps, laughing her head off.

But the kitten wasn't so amused. She took one look at Bullwinkle and leaped out of Patti's arms. She tore up the nearest tree, her balloon ribbon unraveling and drifting into the sky.

The calico climbed to the topmost branch·and stayed there, hissing and spitting at the frolicking monster below.

I turned my balloons loose and threw myself on Bullwinkle.

"Listen, Kate," I said, struggling with Bullwinkle. "We weren't . . . ooof! . . . doing things behind your back, or at least. . . ."

"Well, we kind of were, but it was because. . . ." Stephanie was finding it hard to talk, still hanging onto seven huge balloons.

"We just wanted to surprise . . ." Patti tried grabbing one of Bullwinkle's legs.

"Anyway . . ." Stephanie jumped out of the way.

"Happy birthday!" we all said at once.

"And if you want your birthday present any time soon, please call the fire department," Stephanie added, pointing at the kitten in the tree.

By the time the Riverhurst Fire Department's hook-and-ladder company arrived, Patti and I had wrestled Bullwinkle back into my yard. The firetruck parked next to the Beekmans' oak tree. As we stood on the lawn and crossed our fingers, one of the firemen climbed to the very end of the ladder, reached way out — and grabbed the frightened kitten.

We cheered and clapped until the fireman and the calico were safely on the ground.

"You'd better hang on to this little guy," the fireman said, handing the kitten to Kate.

"*Girl*," Stephanie, Patti, and I said automatically.

Kate hugged the calico kitten. "I really love her — thanks!" she said to us. "And thank you so much, Mr. . . ."

"Warren. Fred Warren," the fireman answered.

"If you don't mind, I think I'll name my kitten ᵢₖₐ," Kate told him.

"Fredericka?" Stephanie said doubtfully. "I don't know if — "

"She's Kate's kitten," Patti pointed out firmly.

"And I've never had a nicer present," Kate said. "Let's go inside, guys, before the pizza gets cold and the ice cream melts."

And then, because we still had so much to tell each other — we'd barely spoken in a week — we decided to make a night of it if we could.

"The first Sleepover Weekend!" Stephanie exclaimed. "What a great idea!"

Mrs. Beekman said she'd been expecting it, and of course we could all sleep over at Kate's house.

My mom was amazed that I even bothered to ask, and the Greens and Jenkinses all gave their permission.

"We'll go get our overnight stuff at my house and be right back," I told Kate.

"Why don't you bring the other kittens, too?" she suggested. "It'll give Fredericka one more night with her brothers and sisters."

Chapter
8

We were in Kate's living room with seven balloons bumping against the ceiling and four kittens racing all over the place. We'd just finished the last of the ice-cream cake.

"I'm so stuffed I can hardly move," Stephanie said.

"Maybe you ought to run around a little — you might feel better," I suggested.

"Oh, Lauren — you're such a jock!" Kate said. "What did you have in mind? Fifty jumping-jacks?"

"Not at all," I replied coolly. "What I had in mind was a lively game of Truth or Dare."

"Sounds good to me," Stephanie said. "What ⬛⬛⬛ rest of you?"

"Sure," said Patti.

"Fine with me — who's it?" Kate asked.

"I thought of it, so I'm it," I said. "Truth or dare, Kate?"

"Truth," Kate answered.

"Okay — were you surprised? Or weren't you?"

Kate grinned. "You bet I was. I spent the whole week thinking the three of you were mad at me for something, or that you just didn't like me anymore . . . until the clown showed up."

"I wish we could have heard him better," Stephanie said. "He really sounded awful."

"She," Kate said. "The clown was a girl."

"You're kidding!" I exclaimed. "Now I know what to tell Aunt Beth when she asks me what I want to be when I grow up."

Stephanie snickered. "Kate, it's your turn."

"Stephanie — truth or dare?"

"Uh — dare. But please don't make it too energetic, okay?"

"It isn't. Call Robert Ellwanger and ask him to go to the movies."

"Oh, no!" Stephanie groaned. "Aren't you ever going to forget that? That was months ago!" At one of our sleepovers, Stephanie had made Kate call Robert and ask him to come over.

Patti and I burst out laughing. "Kate never forgets anything."

"All right . . ." Stephanie said.

"It's not even late." Kate handed her the phone and the phone book. "Ellwanger. Richard. That's his father's name. E-L-L — "

"I know how to spell it," Stephanie said. She found the number and dialed. The phone rang several times. "I think they're all out. Wait . . . Hello?" *His mother*, she mouthed at us. "Is Robert in?"

Mrs. Ellwanger said something.

"May I speak to him? This is Stephanie Green. I'm a fifth-grader at Riverhurst Elementary." She looked at us. "Ick!"

"What are you worrying about? He won't accept," I whispered. "He said no to Kate."

Stephanie waved her hand for us to be quiet. "Hello . . . Robert?" She held the phone so we could all hear. "This is Stephanie Green. I'm in 5B, Mrs. Mead's room?"

"I know that," Robert said. He has a really squeaky voice.

"Oh. You do . . . I was just calling to ask" — Stephanie stopped, and Kate nudged her — "to ask if you'd like to go to the movies next Saturday."

". . . some kind of joke?" Robert squeaked.

70

"Oh . . . no. Not at all," said Stephanie, rolling her eyes.

The rest of us were holding our hands over our noses and mouths, trying not to giggle.

"I'd like that a lot, Stephanie," Robert Ellwanger replied. "What time and at which theater?" He managed to sound nerdy and full of himself at the same time.

Oh, no, Stephanie's lips said, although no sounds came out. "Uh . . . I'll check the schedules and let you know, okay?"

"All right. If I don't hear from you by tomorrow afternoon, I'll give you a call. What's your number?"

"Five-five-five . . . two . . . four . . . seven . . . eight." Stephanie could hardly bring herself to finish it.

"Catch you later," said Robert.

Stephanie hung up.

"Catch you later!" Kate, Patti, and I shrieked.

Stephanie stuck out her tongue. "Okay, Kate — I think we're even about Robert Ellwanger."

"You should feel flattered, Stephanie. He turned Kate down flat," I teased.

"He must like girls with dark, wavy hair," Kate added.

"I think it's your new look," Patti s

But before the game was over, Stephanie got Kate back. I picked Stephanie when it was my turn again. "Truth or dare?" I asked.

"Dare." Stephanie practically always answers *dare*. She says it's more fun.

"I want you to run around Donald Foster's house."

"You have to be kidding me!" she said.

"This *is* 'Truth or Dare,' isn't it?" I replied. "Your cake has had time to settle."

We put the kittens back in their box.

"At least I've got jeans on instead of pajamas," Stephanie said in a low voice as we tiptoed into the kitchen and slowly opened the back door.

"All the way around?" Stephanie whispered.

I nodded. "And don't cheat," I warned.

Stephanie slipped out of the house and dashed across the lawn. She pushed through the hedge and disappeared.

We waited for her to come back — and waited and waited.

"Where is she?" Kate said. "It shouldn't take so long."

We squinted at Donald's house. There wasn't a light on in the place. Minutes passed. We started to get worried.

"She's probably just standing on the other side of the hedge," I said. "If we go look for her, she'll jump out and scare us to death."

"But what if something's wrong?" said Patti.

"We'd better go see," said Kate.

The three of us crept down the steps and sneaked across the Beekmans' yard. We paused at the hedge and listened. Everything was quiet.

"Stephanie?" Patti whispered. "Stephanie!"

There wasn't a sound.

Kate pushed through the hedge . . . and suddenly, four or five voices boomed out, all boys'!

"Happy birthday to you, happy birthday to you, happy birthday, dear Kate, happy birthday to you!"

Flashlights blinked on — it was Donald, Ricky Delman, Larry Jackson — and Royce Mason! Behind them was a tent. They were camping out in the Fosters' backyard. Stephanie had run right into them on her trip around the house!

On one side of us, Bullwinkle started to howl. And on the other Melissa screeched, "Kate — I'm telling Mom!"

The four of us grinned at each other. The Sleepover Friends were back to normal.

America's Favorite Series

THE BABY-SITTERS CLUB®

by Ann M. Martin

The five girls at Stoneybrook Middle School get into all kinds of
adventures...with school, boys, and, of course, baby-sitting!

Collect Them All!

☐ 41985-4	#1 Kristy's Great Idea	$2.75
☐ 41986-2	#2 Claudia and the Phantom Phone Calls	$2.75
☐ 42124-7	#3 The Truth About Stacey	$2.75
☐ 42123-9	#4 Mary Anne Saves the Day	$2.75
☐ 42232-4	#5 Dawn and the Impossible Three	$2.75
☐ 40748-1	#6 Kristy's Big Day	$2.50
☐ 42122-0	#7 Claudia and Mean Janine	$2.75
☐ 42121-2	#8 Boy-Crazy Stacey	$2.75
☐ 41128-4	#14 Hello, Mallory	$2.75
☐ 41588-3	Baby-sitters on Board! Special Edition	$2.95
☐ 41587-5	#15 Little Miss Stoneybrook and Dawn	$2.75
☐ 41586-7	#16 Jessi's Secret Language	$2.75
☐ 41585-9	#17 Mary Anne's Bad Luck Mystery	$2.75
☐ 41584-0	#18 Stacey's Mistake	$2.75
☐ 41583-2	#19 Claudia and the Bad Joke	$2.75
☐ 42004-6	#20 Kristy and the Walking Disaster	$2.75
☐ 42005-4	#21 Mallory and the Trouble with Twins (February, 1989)	$2.75
☐ 42006-2	#22 Jessi Ramsey: Pet Sitter (March, 1989)	$2.75
☐ 42007-0	#23 Dawn on the Coast (April, 1989)	$2.75

REFIX CODE 0-590-

Available wherever you buy books...or use the coupon below.

Scholastic Inc. P.O. Box 7502, 2932 E. McCarty Street, Jefferson City, MO 65102

Please send me the books I have checked above. I am enclosing $_____
(please add $1.00 to cover shipping and handling). Send check or money order–no cash or C.O.D.'s please.

Name_____

Address_____

City_____ State/Zip_____
Please allow four to six weeks for delivery. Offer good in U.S.A. only. Sorry, mail order not available to residents of
Canada.   Prices subject to change.   BSC888